# Rosy Wolf Snails Invade Pacific Islands

By Susan H. Gray

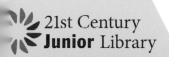

21st Century
**Junior** Library

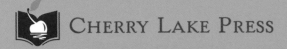

## CHERRY LAKE PRESS

Published in the United States of America by Cherry Lake Publishing Group
Ann Arbor, Michigan
www.cherrylakepublishing.com

Reading Adviser: Beth Walker Gambro, MS, Ed., Reading Consultant, Yorkville, IL
Book Designer: Melinda Millward

Photo Credits: © O'KHAEN/Shutterstock.com, cover, 20; © Liz Weber/Shutterstock.com, 4; © Shane Myers
Photography/Shutterstock.com, 6; © Martin Pelanek/Shutterstock.com, 8; © Milky3115/Shutterstock.com, 10;
© Nedrofly/Shutterstock.com, 12; © karegg/Shutterstock.com, 14; © Klara_Steffkova/Shutterstock.com, 16;
© AnongTH/Shutterstock.com, 18

**Cherry Lake Press** is an imprint of Cherry Lake Publishing Group.

Library of Congress Cataloging-in-Publication Data

Names: Gray, Susan Heinrichs, author.
Title: Rosy wolf snails invade Pacific Islands / by Susan H. Gray.
Description: Ann Arbor, Michigan : Cherry Lake Publishing, 2021. | Series: Invasive species science :
    tracking and controlling | Includes index. | Audience: Grades 2-3
Identifiers: LCCN 2021004887 (print) | LCCN 2021004888 (ebook) | ISBN 9781534187061 (hardcover) |
    ISBN 9781534188464 (paperback) | ISBN 9781534189867 (pdf) | ISBN 9781534191266 (ebook)
Subjects: LCSH: Rosy wolfsnail—Control—Islands of the Pacific—Juvenile literature. | Introduced animals—Islands
    of the Pacific—Juvenile literature. | Invasive species—Control—Islands of the Pacific—Juvenile literature.
Classification: LCC QL430.5.S65 G73 2021 (print) | LCC QL430.5.S65 (ebook) | DDC 594/.38099—dc23
LC record available at https://lccn.loc.gov/2021004887
LC ebook record available at https://lccn.loc.gov/2021004888

Cherry Lake Publishing Group would like to acknowledge the work of the Partnership for 21st Century Learning, a
Network of Battelle for Kids. Please visit http://www.battelleforkids.org/networks/p21 for more information.

Printed in the United States of America
Corporate Graphics

# CONTENTS

Rosy wolf snails use their oral sensory organs to hunt prey.

# Lunch!

A rosy wolf snail glides over a fallen tree limb. **Oral** sensory organs stick out from its head. Nonstop, they move back and forth, up and down. They are tasting something on the limb. It's the slime trail left by a tree snail.

The **predator** speeds up and quickly overtakes the tree snail. This snail is much slower than the rosy wolf snail. The rosy wolf snail attacks and eats its lunch.

More than 70 years ago, the rosy wolf snail was brought to Hawaii.

This scene occurs thousands of times each day in Hawaii. It also takes place in Guam and the Cook Islands. It happens in Tahiti, Samoa, and most other islands in the South Pacific. It has been going on for years. Now, many small snails in these islands are disappearing. Some **species** exist only in zoos. And some are totally **extinct**.

# Ask Questions!

Rosy wolf snails normally live in the southeastern part of the United States. Search online to see what keeps them under control there.

The African snail destroyed crops and gardens in Hawaii.

# One Problem Leads to Another

Hawaiians had **imported** the African snail to **enhance** their gardens. But the giant African snail was eating everything from apples to watermelons.

## Make a Guess!

It takes years for people to realize that some animals are **invasive**. Why does it take so long?

Tree snails are much smaller than rosy wolf snails.

In 1955, the Hawaii Department of Agriculture acted. They brought in some rosy wolf snails and put them where African snails lived. They expected the rosy wolf snails to attack. But the wolf snails weren't interested in the giant snails. They preferred to eat smaller snails. They ate them—shell and all.

## Look!

Find a map of the South Pacific islands. Rosy wolf snails do well in these islands. What sort of climate do you think these snails prefer?

Tree snails help recycle materials in the environment.

# A Tale of Three Snails

Tree snails are important for several reasons. These little animals eat microscopic plants called algae. They eat bits of algae that grow on tree leaves. This keeps the leaves clean and the trees healthy.

Tree snails also chow down on rotting plants and leaves. As they digest this food, it is broken down. It then becomes part of the soil and nourishes new plants.

There are over 40 species of Hawaiian tree snails.

Hawaii—and other Pacific islands—now had three snail problems. The giant African snails were still eating crops. The rosy wolf snails weren't doing anything about it. Plus, now *they* were increasing. And tree snails were quickly disappearing.

Dealing with an invasive species is not easy. Wildlife experts must first decide how bad the problem is. First, they figure out how far the invader has spread. They also study the amount of damage it has caused.

On some islands, tree snails are now protected. **Barriers** surround the trees so rosy wolf snails cannot get in.

The next step is to inform the public. Scientists work with news reporters to do this. Together, they tell people not to import, **export**, or collect invaders.

Experts also talk to government officials. The officials then pass laws forbidding people to import invasive species. This happened in the South Pacific. It became illegal to move rosy wolf snails from one island to another.

Zoos are raising tree snails that would be at risk on their own islands.

# Teamwork Pays Off

**Islanders** work to control the rosy wolf snails. Once it's safe, the zoo snails are flown to their native homes and released.

# Think!

If you had to design a snail barrier, what would it look like?

Rosy wolf snails are one of the worst invasive species in the world.

It will take years to control the rosy wolf snails. But there is hope. Scientists are working with lawmakers. Zoos are working with Pacific Islanders. News reporters are informing the public. Such teamwork is the best way to solve this problem.

# GLOSSARY

**barriers** (BER-ee-uhrs) structures that prevent movement through or past them

**enhance** (en-HANTS) to improve something or make it more attractive

**export** (ex-PORT) to move or take something out of a place

**extinct** (ek-STINGKT) no longer living anywhere in the world

**imported** (im-PORT-ihd) brought in from another place

**invasive** (in-VAY-sihv) not native, but entering by force or by accident and spreading quickly

**Islanders** (EYE-luhn-durz) people who live on an island

**oral** (OR-uhl) having to do with the mouth or with taste

**predator** (PREH-duh-tur) an animal that hunts and eats other animals

**species** (SPEE-sheez) a particular kind of plant or animal

# FIND OUT MORE

## BOOKS

Chung, Liz. *Controlling Invasive Species*. New York, NY: Rosen Publishing, 2017.

Gilles, Renae. *Invasive Species in Infographics*. Ann Arbor, MI: Cherry Lake Publishing, 2020.

Gray, Susan H. *Giant African Snail*. Ann Arbor, MI: Cherry Lake Publishing, 2009.

## WEBSITES

**DK Findout!—Snails**
www.dkfindout.com/uk/animals-and-nature/squid-snails-and-shellfish/snails
Find out more about snails and check out the link to giant African snails.

**Enchanted Learning—Snails**
www.enchantedlearning.com/subjects/invertebrates/mollusk/gastropod/Snailprintout.shtml
Read about snail anatomy and discover which snails are the smallest and largest in the world.

**Man and Mollusk—Rosy Wolf Snail**
http://www.manandmollusc.net/Odessa/rosy.html
Learn all the places where the rosy wolf snail exists and how it eats other snails.

# INDEX

## ABOUT THE AUTHOR

Susan H. Gray has a master's degree in zoology. She has written more than 180 reference books for children and especially loves writing about animals. Susan lives in Cabot, Arkansas, with her husband, Michael, and many pets.